Judy Moody & Stink

The Big Bad Blackout

Books by Megan McDonald
and Peter H. Reynolds

Judy Moody & Stink: The Holly Joliday
Judy Moody & Stink: The Mad, Mad, Mad, Mad Treasure Hunt
Judy Moody
Judy Moody Gets Famous!
Judy Moody Saves the World!
Judy Moody Predicts the Future
Judy Moody: The Doctor Is In!
Judy Moody Declares Independence
Judy Moody Around the World in 8 ½ Days
Judy Moody Goes to College
Judy Moody, Girl Detective
Judy Moody and the NOT Bummer Summer
Judy Moody and the Bad Luck Charm
Judy Moody, Mood Martian
Stink: The Incredible Shrinking Kid
Stink and the Incredible Super-Galactic Jawbreaker
Stink and the World's Worst Super-Stinky Sneakers
Stink and the Great Guinea Pig Express
Stink: Solar System Superhero
Stink and the Ultimate Thumb-Wrestling Smackdown
Stink and the Midnight Zombie Walk
Stink and the Freaky Frog Freakout
Stink and the Shark Sleepover
Stink-O-Pedia: Super Stinky-y Stuff From A to Zzzzz
Stink-O-Pedia 2: More Stinky-y Stuff From A to Z

www.judymoody.com   www.stinkmoody.com

Judy Moody & Stink
The Big Bad Blackout

Megan McDonald

illustrated by Peter H. Reynolds

WALKER
BOOKS

First published in Great Britain 2015 by Walker Books Ltd
87 Vauxhall Walk, London SE11 5HJ

2 4 6 8 10 9 7 5 3 1

Text © 2014 Megan McDonald
Illustrations © 2014 Peter H. Reynolds
Judy Moody font © 2004 Peter H. Reynolds

The right of Megan McDonald and Peter H. Reynolds
to be identified as author and illustrator respectively of
this work has been asserted by them in accordance
with the Copyright, Designs and Patents Act 1988

This book has been typeset in Stone Informal

Printed in China

British Library Cataloguing in
Publication Data: a catalogue
record for this book is available
from the British Library

ISBN 978-1-4063-5345-7

www.walker.co.uk

For Lovey

M. M.

To Eloise and Jack Cheever

P. H. R.

CONTENTS

Crash Landing 11

Elmer 25

Big Bad Blackout 33

Ghost Toasties 45

Hurricane Annabelle 61

Annie Oakley and the Fireman 75

Mr Drybones and the Viper 91

The Ghost of Weejie 103

Up Periscope! 117

The Ghost-Toastie Oath 127

Bump! *Thwump!*

"Ghost!" Judy yelped, bolting awake from a crash on the roof. Her heart beat louder than a ticking clock. "That sounded like a giant bionic squirrel landing on the roof, Mouse. Or all nine of Santa's reindeer."

Mouse covered an ear with one paw.
Ba-bump-bump-bump.

"Eeeeee! What if it *is* a ghost? And he's bowling – up in the attic!" Judy held her cat close. "Don't be scared, Mouse. I'll protect you."

Judy scrambled down from her top bunk and grabbed a Grouchy pencil and her Women of Science ruler. Brandishing one in each hand, she rushed out the door and bumped headlong into…

Stink! He waved a lightsaber and yelled, "The sky is falling! The sky is falling!"

"Hey, Chicken Little! Did you hear what I just heard?" Judy asked.

"If you mean the giant spaceship that just crash-landed on the roof, I heard it." Judy and Stink flew down the stairs, Mouse at their heels. They skidded into the kitchen on sock feet, looking for Mum and Dad.

Computer? On. TV? On. But no Mum or Dad.

Just then, Mum came out of the utility room, tugging on her wellies.

"Ghost!" Judy pointed to the attic with her ruler.

"Spaceship!" said an out-of-breath Stink.

"Bionic squirrel! Reindeer!" Judy spouted.

"Alien! Invasion!" Stink hiccupped.

"Crash landing!" Judy sputtered.

"Roof!" Stink nodded.

"It's this storm," said Mum. "The wind has kicked up like crazy. Dad's outside checking the roof right now." Mum shrugged on her raincoat and grabbed an umbrella. "You kids sit tight. I'm going out to look too." She opened the back door to step out, and a flurry of wet leaves blew in.

"Great," said Stink. "Aliens just crash-landed right here in Frog Neck Lake, Virginia, and we're supposed to sit tight."

☙   ☙   ☙

Rain, rain and more rain. Rain drummed on the roof. Rain hammered against the house. Judy watched it run in rivers down the windows.

When she turned around, Stink had his ear pressed up to a … torch? A talking torch!

"AlleyOop Charter, Clara Barton Elementary, Crabtree Elementary, closed."

"What did the torch say to the second grader?" Judy teased.

Stink looked up. "I don't know? What?"

"It's not a joke, Stink. You're listening to ... a torch?"

"Hardee-har-har. It's a torch, but it's also a radio." He jiggled the antenna. "I'm trying to find out if school's cancelled."

Wind rattled the back door. "It's not a snow day, Stink. Whoever heard of a *rain* day?"

"It could happen," said Stink.

"Yeah, right. And pencils grow on trees."

"Uh … pencils are *made* from trees," said Stink.

"Oh. Right."

"Franklin Elementary, Hall Elementary, closed." Stink crossed his fingers on both hands.

"Say *Virginia Dare Elementary*!" he shouted at the radio.

"It's raining cats and dogs out there," said Mum, coming through the back door, her umbrella turned inside out.

"Any guinea pigs?" Stink asked slyly.

"Dad's still trying to find out what made that awful noise on the roof. I couldn't see a thing."

"Our Lady of Peace School, Plum Creek Middle School, closed."

Dad came in the back door next, dripping a pond-sized puddle on the floor.

"So?" asked Stink. "Was it a spaceship?"

"Or Santa?" said Judy.

"Aliens?"

"Reindeer?"

"Guinea pigs?"

"Tent," said Dad, shaking water from his hair like a dog. "Your Toad Pee Club tent was up on the roof."

"You mean to say the wind picked up the tent and blew it all the way across the garden," Stink said, waving his arms wildly, "and then – *bing, bang, boom!* – up onto the roof?"

"Yep," said Dad.

"Whoa. Crash landing! Just like the house in *The Wizard of Oz*," said Judy.

"Now we'll have to have our club meetings up on the roof!" Stink said with a grin.

"No, I got the tent down," said Dad. "But this is no ordinary storm. Weather report said winds are over sixty kilometres per hour and we've had several centimetres of rain already. Looks like we might be in for a hurricane."

Judy's eyes grew wide.

Stink looked from Dad to Mum.

Dad turned up the TV. "It's official. What we hoped was just a tropical storm has just been upgraded to hurricane status," the weatherman reported. "Batten down the hatches, folks. Hurricane Elmer is heading straight for the East Coast."

"Hurricane!" cried Stink. "Shouldn't we be doing something? Boiling water?"

"That's if a baby's coming, Stink. Isn't it, Mum?"

"Then we should be breathing into a paper bag or something."

"That's for hiccups," said Judy.

"Stand in a doorway?"

"Earthquakes, Stink."

"Silver Lake Middle School, Skipwith Academy, Wee Ones Preschool, closed. This just in: Frog Neck Lake..."

"Shh!" Stink put the torch up to his ear.

"... *Public Library, Frog Neck Lake Senior Centre...*"

"Aw," said Stink. "They're never going to say our school."

"Kids? You'd better get ready," said Mum. "If there is school, you're already going to be late."

"*Frog Neck Lake School District – including Virginia Dare Elementary School – closed.*"

Stink looked at Judy. Judy looked at Stink.

"No school?" Stink asked.

"No school!" said Judy.

"Woo-hoo!" Judy and Stink high-fived, low-fived, middle-fived, and then they danced around the kitchen.

Later that morning, Mrs Moody made a quick trip to the supermarket. When she came back, Stink stood on tiptoe, peering into the bags. "Did you get marshmallows?"

"I got marshmallows," said Mum. "They were out of tuna fish and soup and cereal, but they still had marshmallows. The shelves were almost bare with everybody stocking up for the storm."

"I guess we'll have to eat marshmallow soup," said Judy.

"Mmm. I don't care," said Stink.

"I could *live* in a house of marshmallows."

Dad carried a giant blue water bottle in from the car. "Who lives in a house of marshmallows?" he asked.

"Grandma Lou!" Stink yelled.

"What? Grandma Lou doesn't—" Judy started.

"No, I forgot," said Stink. "I was supposed to tell you guys that Grandma Lou called. She's on her way here to stay with us."

"Good. Because Virginia Beach is getting slammed," said Dad.

"Stink said her power already went out," Judy reported.

"She had to leave or they were going to evaporate her!" said Stink.

"I think it's *evacuate*," said Mum. "I'm glad she left when she did. If they closed the bridge in high winds, she'd be stuck."

"Poor Grandma Lou always seems to be in the teeth of the storm," said Dad.

"And," said Stink, "I'm supposed to tell you she's not alone."

Mum raised an eyebrow at Dad. "Oh?"

"Who's she bringing?" Dad asked.

"Somebody named … Gert. And Pugsy and some other names, too. I can't remember."

"Maybe Grandma Lou has an evil twin named Gert and they were separated at birth and she's bringing her here and Evil Gert will cast an evil spell on us," Judy said all in one breath.

27

Dad laughed. "I hate to break this to you, but Gert is short for *Gertrude*. And *Gertrude* is Grandma Lou's kayak."

"Grandma Lou has a boat named *Gert*?" said Judy.

"See, right before Grandpa Jack died, he told Grandma Lou, 'Whatever you do, don't be an old Gertrude.' So Grandma Lou went out and got herself a kayak. To help her stay young. She named it *Gert*. Short for *Gertrude*."

"Phew," said Stink. "A boat's way better than an evil twin."

Dad turned up the TV. "Sounds like they think Elmer will hit land later tonight on the Outer Banks of North Carolina," he said.

Outside, the wind howled. Mouse leaped from her perch on top of the fridge to the floor and made a dash for the utility room.

"The storm is freaking her out," said Stink.

"Storms and vacuum cleaners," said Judy. "Those make her run and hide in the laundry basket, under all the clothes."

"Not the clean clothes, I hope," said Mum. "Kids? You'll have to bunk together with Grandma Lou coming. Judy, you can sleep in Stink's room for a few nights."

Stink pumped his fist in the air. "Yes, yes, yes!"

"No, no, nooooo," Judy groaned.

"No moaning," said Mum.

"Fine. There's already a ghost in my room, anyway."

"You have a lot to do to get your room cleaned up before Grandma Lou gets here," Mum pointed out.

"Ha ha." Stink was pointing at Judy. "School's out and you have to clean your room!"

"Stink, you need to pick up your room too," said Mum.

"Ha ha to you," said Judy.

"I can't pick up my room," said Stink.

"Why not?" Mum asked.

"It's too heavy!" said Stink. He cracked himself up again.

Beep-beep-beep! Hooonk! Stink and Judy ran to the front window. The rain made a Morse code of dots and dashes on the panes. Wind bent the trees sideways. A yellow Mini had pulled into the driveway. A red kayak was strapped to the roof.

"Grandma Lou's here!" called Judy and Stink.

Holding a newspaper over her head, Grandma Lou made a mad dash for the front door, puddle-jumping and splashing all the way.

"Kiddos!" Grandma Lou squeezed them in a big hug. "Am I glad to see you!"

"Hey! You're getting us all wet," said Stink.

"How was your trip, Mum?" Dad asked.

"Crazy!" said Grandma Lou. "The waves are this high and there's flooding in the streets. Everybody's heading inland, so the bridge was bumper-to-bumper traffic all the way."

"We're glad you're here safe and sound," said Mum. "C'mon in and dry off."

"First things first," said Grandma Lou, and reached into her tote bag. Then she pulled out a wet pug and set him on the floor.

"Pugsy!" cried Judy and Stink. Pugsy shook himself off.

"Kids, keep an eye on Pugs for a minute. Be back in a flash." Grandma Lou dashed back through the rain to her car.

Pugsy jumped and bounced and ran through the kids' legs, playing tag.

"Wonder who else she's brought," Mum said, moving aside the curtain to see.

Grandma Lou came back with a Critter Keeper in each hand. "This is Milo," she said, holding up one of the pet carriers. Two black eyes, a pink nose and a black-and-white striped face peered out.

"P.U.! Skunk!" yelled Stink, pinching his nose shut.

"He's not a skunk. He's a ferret," said Grandma Lou. "And this," she said, holding up the other pet carrier, "is Candy Cane."

"Snake!" yelled Stink. Everybody backed away.

"Don't worry, she's friendly," said Grandma Lou. "She's a corn snake."

"A corn snake named Candy Corn?" Stink asked. "Weird."

"Candy *Cane*," said Judy. "I get it. Because she has red-and-white stripes."

"Somebody sure got pranked when they looked in their Christmas stocking," said Stink. "Hey, wait. The snake's sleeping in your room, right, Grandma Lou?"

"Sure. The snake will make a good foot warmer!" Grandma Lou teased.

"So, you brought a zoo," said Dad. "Anything else we should know?"

"I know. I'm sorry," said Grandma Lou. "I'm pet sitting. My neighbours are waiting out the storm at a shelter that won't take pets, so they asked me to help. I could hardly say no."

"You got skunked!" said Stink.

"You won't even know they're here. I promise."

"A snake in the house? I'll know," Mum teased. "Judy, take Grandma Lou up to your room."

"You carry Milo's cage," said Grandma

Lou. "I'll carry the snake." She followed Judy upstairs.

"These are my bunk beds," said Judy. "You can sleep on the top or bottom. I'll be rooming with Stink." She made a sour-ball face.

"Sorry about that. You're welcome to bunk with me."

"That's OK."

Judy pointed to her bookshelves. "These are my books. You can read them, but if there's a bookmark, don't lose my place."

"I hate it when that happens," said Grandma Lou.

"I'll clear my desk off for Candy Cane," said Judy. "But don't let her get too close to my Venus flytrap. Jaws likes to snap!"

"I'll remember that," said Grandma Lou.

"This is my Band-Aid collection. You can use some, but ask me first. And here's my pizza-table collection – don't let Pugsy chew them, like last time."

Grandma Lou nodded. "I'm sure Pugsy and I will be very comfy."

"*And* Milo *and* Candy Cane," said Judy. "It sure is zooey in here!"

      ◎   ◎   ◎

That afternoon, while Grandma Lou took a nap, Judy and Stink played fetch with Pugsy and Mouse. Judy and Stink took Milo for a walk around the living-room. "How do you play with a snake?" Stink asked.

"You don't," said Judy.

Rain slashed the windows and thrum-drummed on the roof. "The storm is headed straight for Ocracoke," said the TV. "It could hit land in the next few hours."

When Grandma Lou woke up, she helped Judy and Stink write a message in a bottle. It said *Come over after the storm* in secret code.

Judy ran outside and set it free in the storm drain. "It should reach Rocky by tomorrow," she told them.

All of a sudden, the lights blinked. Off. On. Off. On.

Thunder rumbled low like a car engine, and lightning cracked the sky. The lights flickered. The lights dimmed. The lights came back on.

Stink looked at the ceiling. "Grandma Lou? If you're sleeping tonight and you happen to hear a loud crash on the roof, don't be scared. It's probably not aliens."

"Or reindeer," said Judy. "Or a giant bionic squirrel."

"And it's probably not Bigfoot," said Stink. "Just so you know."

"Or Sasquatch. Or the Skunk Ape," said Judy.

"Good to know," said Grandma Lou.

"It's probably just a normal old ghost," Judy teased.

Whoooo! All of a sudden, the lights went out again. The room turned ink black. The TV fell silent. It felt like the house was under a magic spell. Outside, the wind whooshed like waves pounding the shore. Chimes clanged and rain poured.

The scary dark sent chills up Judy's spine.

"Ooh, blackout!" cried Stink. "A big bad blackout!"

Ghost
Toasties

"I'll get the candles," said Mum.

"I'll get the torches," said Dad.

"I'll get the marshmallows!" said Stink.

Outside, the storm flashed and crashed. Pugsy yipped and yapped. Milo ran in circles around the room.

Judy and Grandma Lou felt their way to the front window and peered outside. "The whole street is black," said Judy.

"Looks like the storm knocked out power to the whole neighbourhood," said Grandma Lou.

"Spooky!" said Stink. "No electricity –
no lights, no computer, no TV. That means
– *waah!* – I can't play the *Mad Muskrats*
physics-based castle demolition game."

"No computer mini-golf or bowling
games either," said Judy.

"But also no bath," Stink chirped, "and
no homework!"

Mum brought candles set in tuna-fish
tins to the table.

"We're pioneers," said Stink. "Like Abe
Lincoln in his log cabin! Except instead
of coyotes and mountain lions, there are
ferrets and candy-cane snakes."

Mum went to look for more candles.
Dad started a fire in the fireplace. The
house seemed extra snug in the dark.

Outside, the wind howled.

"I'm bored," said Stink.

"You're not bored," said Judy. "You're never bored."

"I know. But it's dark and nobody's said anything for a while."

"There are lots of things we can do by candlelight," said Grandma Lou. "I could teach you to knit. We could make knitted zombies!"

A tree branch cracked outside the window. Stink shivered. "No, thanks," he said.

"We could play cards. How about Cuckoo Canasta?"

"But we only have three people," said Judy.

"I know," said Grandma Lou. "Let's play a board game."

"Cluedo!" said Judy.

"Too scary," said Stink. "Scrabble?"

"Too long," said Judy. "How about Chinese chequers?"

"You always win," said Stink. "Maybe Frustration?"

"*You* always win," said Judy. "Let's play Sorry!"

"Wow," said Grandma Lou. "I'm *sorry* I caused so much *frustration*. We could be here all night trying to make up our minds."

"Abe Lincoln played marbles," said Stink.

"Tell you what. Let's play Musical Board Games," Grandma Lou said.

"Wha? Huh?" said Judy and Stink.

"Musical Board Games. It's Abe Lincoln approved. You know Musical Chairs? You each get to pick two board games. We'll set up all four games around the room."

"Four games!" said Judy.

"I'll turn on the music and you start playing one game. When I stop the music, you move to the next game. It goes really fast."

"That's cuckoo-berry!" said Stink.

"Cuckoo-berry times four!" said Judy.

"Let's play," said Stink, bouncing up and down. "No. Wait. Can't. There's no power. How are we going to play music?"

Grandma Lou dug in her bag. "One thing you should know about your old grandma. She never leaves home without…"

"A pack of cards?" asked Stink.

"Cough drops?" asked Judy.

"Batteries!"

"Stink, go get Dad's old CD player," Judy said.

Judy and Stink played Musical Board Games till they were out of breath. Pugsy chased after Judy and Stink, and Milo chased after Pugsy. Mouse watched the whole thing. Then they played Spit in the Ocean and Old Maid (which Grandma Lou made them call Not-So-Old Granny).

"Let's read a book," said Grandma Lou.

"It's too dark," said Judy and Stink at the same time.

"Jinx! One - two - three - four - five - six - seven!" said Judy. "You owe me a hot chocolate, Stink!"

"Too bad the stove doesn't work in the blackout. Ha ha!"

Grandma Lou rummaged through her bag and pulled out a book. *"Candlelight Stories!* This was your dad's book when he was your age."

"Coolsville," said Stink. "Abe Lincoln didn't have electricity in his log cabin, so he read books by candlelight too."

Grandma Lou read a fairy tale about a mouse, a bird and a talking sausage! While she read, Stink folded origami boats. Mouse toyed with them. When Judy made a hurricane flip book out of sticky notes, Pugsy tried to chew it.

"Weird!" said Stink. "I bet Abe Lincoln did not have a book about a talking sausage. I never knew it could be so fun without a computer."

"Or lights," said Judy.

"Or a TV or video games," said Stink.

Stink got out his markers and made a poster about nine things to do in a blackout.

Dad tried Stink's torch radio, but he couldn't get a signal. "I'll try the radio in the car." When he came back, he said, "Sounds like they've closed half the streets in town. We may need *Gert* just to get you two to school tomorrow."

"School?" said Judy.

"*School?*" said Stink.

"Just kidding!" said Dad. "Actually, they may need the school for a shelter, so it'll probably be a few days."

"Yippee!" yelled Stink and Judy.

◎   ◎   ◎

When it was time for dinner, Dad asked, "What should we have? Peanut-butter-and-marshmallow sandwiches?"

"I did manage to get bread, eggs and baked beans at the shop," said Mum.

"Silver-dollar pancakes!" said Stink.

"Don't tell me. Abe Lincoln ate silver-dollar pancakes," said Judy.

Stink shrugged. "No. But he did eat corn cakes with honey. And sausages. *Not* the talking kind."

"Breakfast for dinner," said Grandma Lou. "I like it. But I have a better idea."

"What could be better than having silver-dollar pancakes?" Stink asked.

"Ghosts in the Hole," said Grandma Lou.

"Ghosts in the Hole?" Stink asked in a whisper.

"You take a piece of bread and cut out the middle with a biscuit cutter."

"We used to call them Toads in the Hole!" said Dad.

"We did. And I just happen to have" – Grandma Lou rummaged in her bag – "a ghost-shaped biscuit cutter. See? You cook an egg in the middle. We can do it in a frying pan over the fire."

"Ghost toast!" said Judy. "I like it!"

"Ghost Toasties!" said Stink.

In no time, Grandma Lou had whipped up ghost toast for everybody. Pugsy ate the one she dropped on the floor.

"My Ghost Toastie is staring at me with a creepy yellow eye," said Stink. "I call it the Eye of the Storm." He stabbed a fork into the Eye of the Storm. Yellow stuff oozed all over his plate. "Dinner, I mean breakfast, is better cooked over a fire. Pass the beans, please." He picked up a spoon, dug in and ate beans right out of the tin.

"Stink, you've never liked beans before," said Mum.

"They taste better in a tin," said Stink. "Just like how Abe Lincoln ate them."

"Stink, Abe Lincoln didn't even have food in a tin. Did he?" Judy asked.

"Yah-huh," said Stink. "They ate stuff from tins in the Civil War. Some guy even invented the tin-opener back then."

"Yes, but did Abe Lincoln eat *breakfast* for *dinner*?" said Judy.

"No matter how great he was," said Stink, "I bet even Abe Lincoln never ate Ghost Toasties while he waited out a hurricane."

Dinner was over. The Moodys huddled around the fireplace. Orange and blue flames licked the logs, sending spooky shadows dancing across the family room. Outside, the rain made a steady drumbeat on the roof.

"Is it time yet?" asked Stink.

"Is it time yet?" asked Judy.

"It's time," said Mum.

"Time for what?" asked Grandma Lou.

"Time for s'mores!" yelled Judy and Stink. "Toasted marshmallow sandwiches!"

Dad got the long forks.
Mum got the chocolate
and biscuits. Stink and
Judy ripped open the
marshmallows.

While they roasted marshmallows on
sticks over the fire, Grandma Lou said,
"S'mores go better with stories. Let's each
tell a story."

"You first, Grandma Lou," said Stink.
"And make it scary. But not too scary."

"Hmm, let's see," said Grandma Lou.
"Oh, I know. Well, this story isn't scary,
but it *is* about a hurricane."

"Hurricane story. Cool beans," said Judy.

"When I was a young girl, a little older
than Judy, I lived on a farm and—"

"Is this an olden days story?" asked
Stink. "Like in Abe Lincoln times?"

"Or an LBS like Dad tells?" said Judy.
"A Long Boring Story."

"Thanks a lot," said Dad.

"Did you have electricity back then?"
Stink asked Grandma Lou. "Because Abe
Lincoln didn't."

"Yes, we had electricity," said Grandma
Lou. "I'm not quite as old as Abe Lincoln,
you know. Anyway, my dad – your great-
grandpa – let me raise chickens for my
Young Farmers Club project. I belonged to
the Cluck Club."

"Bwaaaack!" Stink clucked. "Bwack,
bwack."

"I had six chickens. One of them –

Suzie Q – was very special. When she was just a three-day-old chick, I rescued her from the jaws of our barn cat, Daisy."

"Oopsy-Daisy!" said Judy, and everybody cracked up.

"Suzie Q had blue legs and black tail feathers. I had to hand-feed her because she had a crooked beak. That chicken rode around with me on my bike. She'd hop on my shoulder when I was brushing our horse, Sweet Potato, or read with me.

"I'll never forget the first time she laid an egg. She stood up straight as a statue, raised her head high and – oopsy-daisy – looked as surprised as anyone when out popped a monster egg. Not just any old white egg, either. A blue egg!"

"Whoa. Like an Easter egg?" Stink asked.

"Yes, sirree. That bird laid the most beautiful sky-blue egg you ever set eyes on. I knew right then and there Suzie Q would win me a prize at the county fair.

"Then it happened. One warm autumn day – October 1954, I think it was – wind started whipping around the farm like crazy, blowing over anything that wasn't nailed down. We heard on the radio that Hurricane Annabelle was headed our way.

"Boy, that was some storm. Rained like a river. One-hundred-and-ninety-kilometres-per-hour winds.

Took the roof right off our tool shed" – Grandma Lou snapped her fingers – "just like that."

At almost the exact same time as Grandma Lou snapped her fingers, the shutters slapped against the house. Stink jumped.

"Hurricanes are serious business," said Grandma Lou. "Up north in Hampton, people had reported winds of over two hundred kilometres per hour. So you can imagine, when Hurricane Annabelle blew in, I was worried about my chickens. Chickens don't even like to get wet."

"Makes them madder than a wet hen," said Dad, laughing at his own joke.

"All the chickens scurried into the coop, except for one."

"Uh-oh," said Judy.

Grandma Lou nodded. "It was my Suzie Q. I looked everywhere for her. By that time I was as wet as a drowned rat. My dad made me go back inside the house."

"So what'd you do?" Judy asked.

"I pressed my nose to the window, my eyes glued on that chicken coop, hoping she'd come back. I was really angry with my dad for leaving Suzie out there and not letting me go back outside. I'm sure I hardly said three words to him for a whole week!"

"What happened? What happened?"

Stink asked. "Did you ever find her?"

"I went to bed. Hardly slept a wink. Woke up the next morning and everything was blown to smithereens. Tree branches had been tossed around like pick-up sticks. The tool shed was just a pile of toothpicks."

Mum held her breath.

"The chicken coop was gone!"

"What do you mean gone?" Judy asked.

"G-O-N-E gone. Blown from here to Hullabaloo or Timbuktu by Annabelle."

"And Suzie Q?"

"For days after Hurricane Annabelle blew out, I rode around in the back of my dad's truck, searching high and low

69

for that chicken, calling for her, asking everybody we came across if they'd seen a blue-legged, black-tailed chicken with a crooked beak."

"Did you ever find her?" Judy asked.

"Just when I thought I'd never see Suzie Q again, one day, out of the blue, I picked up the newspaper. Right there on the front page was a story about a girl a few

DAILY NEWS

Hen Wins First Prize at County Fair

towns over who had won first prize at the county fair for a blue egg! The paper said she'd found her prize egg-layer in the hurricane, so they called their blue-legged, black-tailed chicken Annabelle.

"I knew Annabelle had to be my Suzie Q. I could tell by her crooked beak. Not to mention she'd got herself a first-prize blue ribbon for laying the most beautiful blue egg."

"Did you get her back?" Judy asked.

Grandma Lou's face glowed copper in the firelight. She smiled. "My daddy drove me out there and we met that girl and her family and I'll be gobsmacked if that chicken didn't flap right up onto my shoulder as soon as she saw me.

"I got my Suzie Q back. To this day, I still can't figure out how she ended up a whole three towns over. But that was the power of Hurricane Annabelle."

"The end," said Stink. "That was a long story."

"And it wasn't even boring!" said Judy.

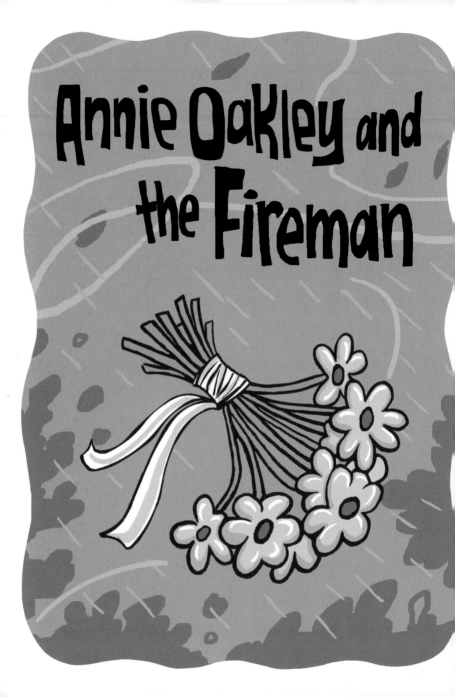

Annie Oakley and the Fireman

Stink stabbed a marshmallow with his fork. "Let's have *some more* stories with s'mores," he chirped.

Mum smiled at Dad over her glasses. "Dad and I have a story. About our wedding."

"It's the story of how another woman came between us," Dad teased.

Stink's eyes got big. "You mean Mum almost wasn't *Mum*?"

"And *you* almost weren't born," Judy teased.

"Her name was Stacy," said Dad.

"Yech," said Stink.

"*Hurricane* Stacy!" Mum cried.

"Hurricane *Cupid*," said Grandma Lou. She winked.

"Tell us. Tell‑us‑tell‑us‑tell‑us!" said Stink.

"For the record, an outdoor wedding was your mother's idea," Dad began.

"The day *started out* warm and sunny," said Mum.

"Then all of a sudden," Dad said, "about an hour before the wedding was supposed to begin, the temperature dropped and the wind kicked up. The whole sky went dark."

"Those dark clouds were like a sign,"

said Mum. Stink shuddered as wind howled down the chimney. A prickle went up Judy's back.

"Trees were bending sideways, and all the chairs on the lawn blew over," Dad told them. "By that time, about sixty or seventy guests had already arrived."

"Then the sky opened up," said Mum. "Rain like you've never seen. And I was in my dress! I ran for shelter under the big white tent, where the tables and food were set up for the reception."

"Did Dad see you?" Judy asked. "That's way bad luck!"

"I'll say. I thought the whole wedding was off!" said Mum. "But Dad suggested we have the wedding under the tent too. Dad and Grandpa Jack rushed to town to get emergency supplies like torches and batteries, in case the power went out."

"Bad idea," said Dad, shaking his head.

"The roads were flooding," said Grandma Lou. "There were downed power lines, fallen trees. It was dangerous to be driving around in that."

"So what happened?" asked Stink.

"CRRASHH!" Mum slapped her hands together like a thunderclap. "The rain came down even harder and blew in sideways under the tent. Me and

Grandma Lou and my parents and the
guests started moving the food from the
tent into the old barn. We had saved
most of it when – *ker-plunk!* – down came
the whole tent."

"Whoa," said Judy.

"By that time, I was drenched," said Mum, "and my dress was ruined. I looked around the barn for something dry to wear. All I could find was a trunk with some old costumes in it."

"Did you dress up like a witch?" Stink asked.

"Or Wonder Woman?" Judy asked.

"Wild West star Annie Oakley," said Mum. Dad cracked up.

"That's cuckoo-berry!" Stink said.

"That's still not the worst part," said Mum.

"What's the worst part?" asked Judy.

"How can it get any worse?" asked Stink.

"No Dad," said Mum.

Judy twisted a curl of hair. Stink tore at a fingernail.

"Three o'clock. Four o'clock. Five o'clock," said Mum. "Still no Dad."

"Did you get scared to marry Mum and run away?" Stink asked Dad.

"Of course not!" said Dad.

"Did you think Dad had ditched you, Mum?" Judy asked.

"It did cross my mind," said Mum. She twirled her wedding ring back and forth. "But mostly I was scared to death that something had happened to him."

"The power had gone out too, of course," said Grandma Lou. "No lights, no microphone, no music."

"No wedding," said Mum. "We were all holed up in the barn, just waiting, listening to the storm rage, when –
Blammo! – off blew the barn doors!
 I remember seeing bits of prawn cocktail bobbing and floating like rubber duckies in a puddle."

Dad tossed another log on the fire. Sparks danced up the chimney.

Stink was practically jumping out of his skin. "Dad! Where were you?"

Dad just smiled. "Let Mum tell it."

Mum went on. "I was sure the whole barn was going to blow down like a house of cards. I mean, everything else had gone kaplooey, right? That's when, above the howling wind, I heard a siren.

It grew closer. And closer. Finally, a fire engine came screaming up the drive. My heart jumped into my throat. I was sure they were coming to tell us that something bad had happened to Dad and Grandpa Jack."

The room got quiet, except for the spitting fire.

"From a loudspeaker on the fire engine came a voice like Darth Vader. The voice said, 'Kate Edison. Will you marry me?'" Mum's eyes teared up. "I raced out into the pouring rain in my Annie Oakley costume. There was your father, leaning off the fire engine, wearing a giant yellow raincoat, a *Little Mermaid* life jacket and a funny grin."

"You had to mention the life jacket, didn't you?" Dad said, chuckling.

"I burst out crying. I was never so happy to see your dad."

"Grandpa and I had driven the car through some deep water in the road and the engine conked out," Dad explained. "We pushed the car to higher ground and tried for ever to get it started. Luckily some firefighters stopped to help. When I said it was my wedding day, well, the rest is history."

Grandma Lou clapped her hands. "Now you kids know the story of how Annie Oakley married a fireman." Stink and Judy laughed.

"So you got married and had us and

lived happily ever after?" said Stink.

"And … we had cake," said Dad.

"Lots and lots of cake," said Mum. "It was about the only thing that didn't get ruined that day. And the fire engine played its radio over the loudspeaker so Dad and I could have our first dance together."

"The Temptations. 'I Wish It Would Rain'." Mum and Dad started singing.

"That's a terrible, horrible, no good, very bad story," said Judy. "But the ending makes it so great!"

"Epic!" said Stink. "Hey, wait. Did you say Edison? That's *my* middle name."

"I thought it was Earwig," said Judy.

"Hardee-har-har." Stink made a face

at Judy. "Too bad the *real* Thomas Edison didn't come to your wedding. He could have invented the lightbulb all over again and saved the whole entire wedding!"

Judy snorted.

"From a whirlwind romance to a hurricane wedding," said Grandma Lou.

Stink held out a cushion. "Kate, Kate, will you marry me? *Mww, mww, mww.*" He made smooching sounds.

Judy hung a pillow-case from her head for a veil and pretended she was in a wedding march. "Da, da, dah-dah," she sang.

"We still have a piece of that wedding cake," said Mum. "In the freezer."

"*That's* the iceberg at the back of the freezer?" Judy asked.

"What are we waiting for?" Stink asked. "Let's eat it."

"We're saving it for a special occasion," said Dad.

"But this is an emergency," said Stink. "What could be more special than that?"

"My turn," said Judy. "I know a hurricane story. It's called Mr Drybones. But it's a little scary." She peered at Stink.

"Why are you looking at me?" Stink asked. "I'm not scared." He scooched closer to Grandma Lou. She put an arm around him.

"Once there was a hurricane named Elmer that came to Frog Neck Lake, Virginia. The winds blew – *woooooh* – and all the lights went out."

"Just like us!" said Stink.

"Down a dark, dark street called Croaker Road, there was a dark, dark house."

Stink leaned in closer. "That's our house!"

"And the dark, dark house had a dark, dark door. Behind the dark, dark door was a dark, dark hall. And down the dark, dark hall were some dark, dark stairs."

Stink shivered. He twisted the end of a blanket into a tornado of a knot.

"At the top of the dark, dark stairs was an even darker hall. At the end of that dark, dark hall was an even darker door."

Before Judy could say the next line of her story, a door slammed. For real!

Everybody jumped. "It's just the wind,"
said Dad. Mouse hid under the sofa.

"Behind the dark, dark door," Judy went
on, "were dark, dark stairs that went up to a
dark, dark attic. In the dark, dark attic was
a dark, dark cupboard. And in the dark,
dark cupboard was a dark, dark box."

"What's in the box?" Stink asked, his
eyes wide.

"From the dark, dark box came a dark,
dark rattling sound, like the sound of
dry bones. And when the dark,
dark box was opened,
out came…"

Stink covered
his eyes with his hands.
"Mr Drybones?" he squeaked.

"No – a pink jelly bean!" Judy squealed. Everybody laughed.

"That's a good one," said Dad. "You had *me* a little scared for a minute."

"I wasn't scared. I wasn't scared!" said Stink.

"Sure, Stink," said Judy.

Dad put one last log on the fire. Grandma Lou pulled a blanket up around Stink's shoulders.

"My turn!" said Stink.

"Let's hear your story, Stink," said Mum. "Then bedtime. It's almost ten. Abe Lincoln was in bed every night by nine o'clock," she added slyly.

"For real?" Stink asked.

"It has to be a hurricane story," Judy told him.

"Um, OK, it's a hurricane story," said Stink. "But it's also an Abe Lincoln story."

"Oh brother," said Judy. "Did they even have hurricanes back then?"

"Yeah. Even Christopher Columbus had one," said Stink.

"It's true," said Dad. "On one of his voyages to the New World."

"And don't forget Ben Franklin," said Mum. "He went out to study an eclipse one night and ended up studying a hurricane."

"Sorry I asked!" said Judy. "I thought it was a day *off* from school, that's all."

"So. Is everybody ready or not?" asked Stink.

"Ready, Freddy," said Judy.

"Once upon a time, Abe Lincoln sat in his log cabin, reading a book."

"Don't tell me. By candlelight," said Judy.

"By candlelight. There was a monster storm outside. We're talking super bad, like it could have been Hurricane Hercules.

Abe rocked back and forth, back and forth in his rocking chair, reading, when… *Brrinngg!*"

Judy jumped.

"The phone rang," said Stink.

"Wait," said Judy. "Abe Lincoln had *a phone*?"

Grandma Lou put her finger to her lips. "Let's let Stink have his turn."

Stink pretended to pick up a phone. "'Hello?' Abe said. A spooky voice on the other end said, 'The Viper is coming, the Viper is coming. The Viper is just down the road.'

"'Who is the Viper? And why are you coming?' Abe asked.

"*Click.* The phone went dead.

"Abe went back to reading. But he hadn't even read two sentences when – *Brrinngg!* – the telephone rang again. 'Helllooo?' Abe said, all shaky-like.

"'The Viper is coming. The Viper is coming for you. The Viper is on your street.'

"Presidents are always super brave, but even tall Abe was a little scared now. 'Who is the Viper? And why are you coming for me?'

"*Click.* The phone went dead. Again.

"Abe was super-scared now. He rocked back and forth, back and forth in his rocking chair when – *Brrinngg!* – the phone rang. *Again.*"

"Not again," said Judy.

"'Not again!' said Abe. He picked up the phone. 'Helllooo?'

"'The Viper is coming. The Viper is

coming. The Viper is almost at your door.'

"Now Abe was shaking in his slippers, he was so scared. But before he could ask, 'Who is the Viper?' one more time, he heard a loud *Boom! Boom! Boom!*

"It wasn't a Toad Pee tent that had landed on his roof. It wasn't a spaceship or a bionic squirrel, either. It was a knock. On his door!" Stink paused. He looked right at Judy. In a spooky voice, he asked, "Should Abe answer the door?"

"Yes!" yelled Judy. "No, wait. No!"

"No. Of course not. But if Abe wanted to be president someday, he had to be brave. So he got up and opened the door a crack. *CREEEAK!*

"Abe peeked out the door. There on his doorstep was a short, funny-looking man with a bucket in one hand and a sponge in the other."

"Sponge Bob?" Judy whispered.

Stink's eyes grew wide. He shook his head no. He threw out his hands and shouted, "'I am the Viper!'"

Everybody jumped. Mouse leaped from under the sofa into Judy's arms. Judy let out a squeal.

"'Who are you?' said Abe. 'And what do you want with me?'

"'I told you. I am the Viper. The Vindow Viper. I come to vipe your vindows!'"

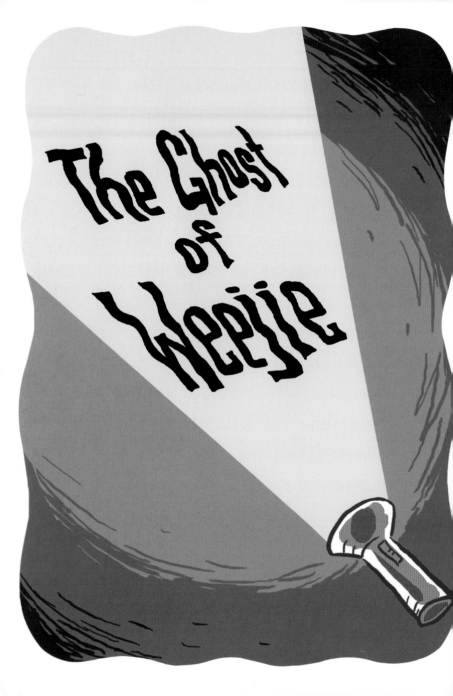

The Ghost of Weejie

The next morning, when Judy came downstairs, Stink was sprawled on the floor writing in a notebook with his five-in-one torch pen.

"What are you doing?" Judy asked.

"Writing a novel," said Stink. "With my hurricane pen – it has a built-in torch. The power's still out. My book's going to be thirty-nine pages long. Want to hear?"

"Sure!" said Judy. She sat down. She closed her eyes and got ready to listen

with her best third-grade listening ears
that she usually saved for school days.

Stink began. "'It was a dark and
stormy night.'"

Silence. More silence. Judy opened
one eye. She opened the other eye.

"Go on," said Judy. "I'm listening."

"That's all I have so far," said Stink.

"Only thirty-eight and three-quarters
more pages to go," said Judy.

"Thirty-eight and a half," said Stink,
"if I write really big."

"Where's Grandma Lou?"

"Everybody's out in the car," said
Stink. "Listening to the radio."

Mum and Dad came back in. "No
school again today," said Mum.

"Yes!" Stink pumped his arm in the air.

"Good news," said Dad. "They downgraded the storm from Category Three to Category Two."

☙ ☙ ☙

Hurricane Elmer. Day two. Grandma Lou taught Judy how to knit with just her fingers. She showed Stink how to mummy-wrap his own hands. They had stare-down contests. They had thumb-wrestling contests. Then Grandma Lou pulled out her fortune-telling game.

"You brought your Ouija board!" said Judy.

"What's a weejie board?" asked Stink.

"It's not for scaredy-cats," said Judy. "It's for talking to ghosts. And for telling fortunes."

"And it glows in the dark," said Grandma Lou. "You kids go ahead and play while I finish my knitting."

"So how does it work?" asked Stink, leaning in to see.

"We rest our fingers on the pointer – lightly – and ask it a question. Then it spells out the answer. Or it says *Yes*, *No* or *Goodbye*."

Judy and Stink placed their fingertips on the pointer. "Me first," said Stink. "What is Judy's middle name?" The pointer spelled out letters one by one.

R-A-T F-A-C-E.

"*Rat face!* No fair, Stink. You made it say that," said Judy.

"Did not!"

"OK," said Judy. "My turn. What is Stink's middle name?"

"P..."

"Wrong! My middle name starts with an E."

The pointer moved to the letter *U.* "P-U," said Judy.

"P-U what?" said Stink.

"That's it. P.U. is your middle name, Stinker."

"Is not," said Stink. "You made it spell that."

Judy shrugged. "I have a question for

real. Will we have school tomorrow?"

The pointer zoomed up to the right-hand corner of the board, where the word *NO* was printed. "NO," said Judy.

"YAY!" said Stink.

"Stink, quit moving it."

"I'm not—"

"Guess what, kids," said Mum, coming into the room. "No school tomorrow either. I just got a robo-call on my mobile phone from the school office."

Judy and Stink locked eyes. Judy got goose bumps. Stink shivered.

"We already know," said Stink. "A ghost just told us."

"The Ghost of Weejie," said Judy.

"Any chance your ghost could tell us when the power's coming back on?" Mum asked, raising an eyebrow.

"OK," said Judy. "But, Stink, you can't move it this time."

"I won't! Cross my heart and spit in my eye!"

"Grandma Lou," said Judy, "will you watch to make sure Stink doesn't move the pointer?"

"OK," said Grandma Lou. "But make it quick. It's almost time for my nap."

"Weejie," said Stink, "is there a ghost in Judy's room?"

Just then, Mouse pounced on the board and the pointer slid down to *GOODBYE*.

"That doesn't count," said Stink. "Mouse moved it."

"OK. Try again."

"Is there a ghost in Judy's room?" Stink asked.

The pointer moved towards the number two. Then the pointer went to the letter *M*. After that it made a beeline for the word *YES*.

"I didn't move it," said Stink. "Honest."

"Me either." Judy's eyes grew wide. "Grandma Lou, I wouldn't take a nap if I were you. Weejie says there's a ghost in my room. And you're sleeping in there."

"I'm not afraid of a silly old ghost," said Grandma Lou.

"You're not?" Judy asked.

"Nope. I grew up in an old house with a ghost."

"You did?" Stink asked.

"Sure. His name was Bob. He liked pretzels."

"Bob? Ghosts don't have the name Bob," said Judy.

"Why not? What name do you think they have? Casper?"

"I don't know. Ichabod. Or Bloody Mary or something."

"Or Abe Lincoln," said Stink. "Some people think his ghost is in the White House. But ghosts aren't real. And they definitely don't eat pretzels."

"How do you know, if you've never seen one?" said Grandma Lou with a twinkle in her eye. "If Santa likes biscuits, why can't Bob like pretzels?"

Stink scratched his head. Stink scratched his elbow. Suddenly, Stink felt itchy and scratchy all over.

"Yep, old One-Legged Bob. We'd hear him clomping around the attic at night, dancing on one leg. Could hardly sleep a wink some nights."

"You're just saying that," Stink said to Grandma Lou.

"Am I?"

"Did Bob ever go bowling up there?" Judy asked.

Stink shook off a shiver. "Dad!" he
called to the next room. "Grandma Lou's
teasing us with scares. About ghosts."

Dad poked his head into the room.
"Grandma Lou sure is a good storyteller,
isn't she, kids?"

"Now I'm going to warm up some milk over the fire and go upstairs to take my nap," said Grandma Lou.

Naps. Ghosts. Pretzels. She, Judy Moody, had an idea.

Rare!

$\int$udy hurry-up whispered her idea to Stink. They raced upstairs.

"Stink, go get a pair of Dad's shoes. And your hurricane pen. And some pretzels. Hurry, before Grandma Lou comes up to take her nap."

Stink didn't even mind Judy bossing him around. Pranking Grandma Lou was going to be even better than the Fake Hand in the Toilet joke.

Judy got the periscope from her room – the one she had made from coffee tins,

oatmeal containers and tissue boxes –
and leaned it up against the wall in the
hall so it would be ready. Next, she tied a
piece of thread to a single pretzel and put
it with other pretzels on a plate on the
bedside table. She flicked the five-in-one
pen to make sure it worked.

She, Judy Moody, with Stink's help,
was going to ghost Grandma Lou good.

"Hey, how about sound effects?" Stink
said, coming back with Dad's boots.
"I have a bunch on the computer."

"Stink. Blackout. Remember? We'll
have to make our own sound effects. Go
get one of Mum's fancy water glasses –
but don't let her see you take it."

Judy and Stink rigged up the greatest

ghost trick ever. Then they hid in Stink's room and waited. Stink could hear Judy breathing. It sounded a little like a ghost. A chill crept across his back.

"I think I hear her," said Stink.

"Shh! Here she comes."

Grandma Lou went into Judy's room and closed the door. Judy and Stink counted to a hundred. Twice.

"Ghost time!" Judy whispered. She motioned Stink to follow her into the hallway.

Stink made one-legged clomping sounds outside Judy's room with a boot of Dad's. Judy scratchy-scratch-scratched on the wall and tappa-tap-tapped on the bedroom door.

No answer. Grandma Lou must have fallen asleep.

"I don't think she heard our ghost," Judy whispered.

Stink mimed opening the door a little. Judy turned the knob and slowly opened the door a crack. Stink made creaky-door sounds with his best squeaky-door voice, as if a ghost were entering the room.

Judy pushed her periscope through the crack. She spied on Grandma Lou.

"Milo, Candy Cane, did you hear something?" they heard Grandma Lou ask. "No? I guess it was just my imagination."

"Cue the ghost," whispered Judy.

Stink wet his finger with spit and rubbed it around the rim of the fancy water glass. *Weeeee! Wooooo!* The glass made ghosty, goose-bumpy sounds. Even Judy got the shivers.

"Did you hear *that?*" they heard Grandma Lou ask the animals. "No? OK. I guess I'll go back to sleep."

"Cue the pretzel," Judy whispered. Stink oh-so-carefully pulled on the end of the string. *CRASH!* The whole plate of pretzels fell to the floor, except for one. One pretzel walked across the floor and out the door.

"A walking pretzel? Now that's strange," they heard Grandma Lou say. "Unless it's a... No. Couldn't be."

And now for the icing on the cake,
thought Judy. Stink handed her his
torch pen. Judy switched it on. A small
green beam of light shot out like a laser.
Through the open crack in the door, Judy
slowly spelled out three letters on the wall
of her room for Grandma Lou to see.

B-O-B.

"Ghost!" they heard Grandma Lou
screech. "Ghost in the house! Bob is back!"

Through the periscope, Judy saw
Grandma Lou jump up in bed.

"Quick! Hide the stuff!" she whisper-
yelled to Stink. Stink tossed the ghost
supplies into his room. Judy tried to hide
the periscope behind her back.

Grandma Lou grabbed Milo and

Candy Cane and dashed out into the hall, almost crashing into Judy and Stink.

"Grandma Lou," said Judy, "you look like you just saw a ghost!"

"G-g-ghost!" Grandma Lou pointed towards Judy's room. "It's Bob. He's baaaaack!"

"Ghost? There's no such thing as ghosts," said Stink.

"Pretzels don't just up and walk by themselves," hissed Grandma Lou. "I told you, ghosts *love* pretzels."

Judy snickered. Stink bit his cheeks to keep from laughing.

Grandma Lou narrowed her eyes. "Wait just a ghost-pretzel-eatin' second.

I see a ghost and – why aren't you two scared? You're up to something, aren't you?"

Judy shook her head. Stink tried to keep a straight face. But he couldn't hold it in for one more second.

"It was us!" Stink cried.

CHOMP! Judy bit into a pretzel and grinned.

"The pretzel-eating ghost is Judy. And me!" Stink cried. "We pranked you! We ghost-pranked you so good!" Judy and Stink rolled on the ground, laughing.

Hummm. Click. Purrrr. Stink woke with a start. Something was different. Something was not right. "Judy!" he said rubbing his eyes. "Did you hear sounds?"

"Umm. Ghost," said a sleepy Judy.

"It's not a ghost. I hear humming. And clicking."

"House sounds, Stink. Go back to sleep."

Stink reached over and flipped a switch. The light blinked on-off-on-off.

"Hey!" Judy said, squinting.

"Power's back on," said Stink. "No more blackout!"

They padded into the hall. Mum and Dad were up too. "We left some lights and things on when the power went out," said Mum.

"I'll check downstairs," said Dad. "You kids go back to bed."

"But I'm not sleepy now," said Stink. "It's too exciting!"

"It's the middle of the night, Stink," said Judy, yawning.

"Warm milk?" Mum asked.

Everybody piled downstairs. Mum heated milk – not on the fire. Judy read her book – not by candlelight. Stink flipped the light switch. On, off. On, off. On. Because he could.

"Yes, Stink. Electricity is a wonderful thing," said Mum. "But don't waste it."

"Think of all the stuff we did this week without electricity," said Judy.

"Are you kidding?" said Stink. "Lights and stuff are like the greatest invention ever. Thank you, Thomas Edison." Blink-blink. Blink-blink-blink.

☉   ☉   ☉

Grandma Lou slept through all the excitement. When she came downstairs in the morning, it had stopped raining and the sky was clearing. "Know what I love most about the storm being over?" she said.

"The *Mad Muskrats* physics-based castle demolition game?" said Stink.

"A warm bubble bath?" said Mum.

"No more beans in a tin?" said Dad.

"It's *after* the storm clears." Grandma Lou nodded at the window. A watery sun shone through the clouds. "Just look up at the sky. I bet you'll see a—"

"Rainbow!" Stink called.

"Double rainbow!" Judy called.

Judy, Stink and Grandma Lou rushed outside. They blinked in the cloudy-bright light. Tree branches and snapped twigs littered the lawn. The roof of the shed had peeled back like a cereal-box top. The letter box had turned into a twisty straw.

Judy tilted her head to the sky. "A double rainbow is way lucky. Luckier than a lucky penny."

"Make a wish," said Grandma Lou.

"I wish we could go out in the kayak," said Judy.

"Yeah, I wish we could go for a ride in *Gert* before Dad makes us clean up the garden," said Stink.

"Follow me," said Grandma Lou.

Before you could say *It was a dark and stormy night*, Grandma Lou, Judy and Stink had slipped into life jackets and were paddling around a "lake" in the back garden. Ducks floated in puddles and frogs kicked up a chorus.

"I can't believe we're in a boat – on a

lake in the middle of the back garden!"
said Stink. "Pretend we're surfing the
rapids on a river in the Grand Canyon."

"How's it feel?" asked Grandma Lou.

"Like I'm a bath toy."

"It's like we're floating on a river of
chocolate milk," said Judy.

"The stream swelled up so high,
it flooded the back garden," said
Grandma Lou.

Stink pointed to a shoe floating past.
"Hey! Isn't that my trainer?"

"And there's my football," said Judy.
"The pink-and-black one that's been up
on the roof since last summer!"

"We're lucky," said Grandma Lou.
"People lose cars, houses, pets in these

storms. One year the wind was so bad, my neighbour's playhouse ended up in a tree."

"A tree house!" said Stink.

"I know the storm's over – and we should be happy that it wasn't a lot worse – but I feel sadder than ABC gum on the bottom of the pool," Judy said.

"I feel bluer than a mutant frog," said Stink.

"Sorry to hear that," said Grandma Lou. "Want to talk about it?"

"It's over," said Stink. "No more storm."

"No more blackout," said Judy.

"It was fun without electricity. But now there will never be another Hurricane Elmer," said Stink.

"Back to school," said Judy.

"And homework," said Stink.

"And now you and Pugsy'll be going home too, Grandma Lou," said Judy.

"Everybody will go back to watching TV and playing games on the computer like we did before," said Stink. "No more stories. No more s'mores."

"Tell you what," said Grandma Lou. "You can come visit me any time, and we'll have a Great Big Blackout of our own. We'll turn out all the lights and cook over a fire and tell stories and eat beans straight out of the tin."

"It'll be just like Earth Hour!" said Judy.

"What's Earth Hour?" Stink asked.

"It's when millions of hundreds of

people all over the world turn out the lights on purpose at the same time for one hour," said Judy.

"To show that we can work together to save energy," said Grandma Lou.

"They even turn out the lights on Big Ben and the Empire State Building and the Eiffel Tower and—"

"OK, Judy. I get it!" said Stink.

"Dare to save the planet, Stink," said Judy.

"I will if you will," said Stink. He turned to Grandma Lou. "But we don't have to wait for Earth Hour, do we?"

"We can have our own Earth Hour too," said Grandma Lou.

"Or Earth *Two* Hours," said Judy.

"With stories and s'mores?" Stink asked.

"And Musical Board Games and everything?" said Judy.

"But no ghosts," said Stink.

"No ghosts," agreed Grandma Lou.

"Not even Ghost Toasties?" Judy asked.

"Well, maybe Ghost Toasties," said Grandma Lou.

"Do you swear?" asked Stink. "On *Gert*?"

Judy and Stink put their heads together and whispered.

"Grandma Lou," said Judy, "Stink and I would like you to take the Ghost-Toastie Oath."

"The Ghost-Toastie Oath, huh?"

"Raise your right hand," said Judy.

Grandma Lou put down her paddle and raised her right hand.

"Repeat after us," said Stink.

"I, Grandma Louise Moody," said Judy.

"I, Grandma Louise Moody," said Grandma Lou.

"Do solemnly swear," said Judy.

"Do solemnly swear," said Grandma Lou.

"That we will have a fake great big blackout…"

"That we will have a fake great big blackout…"

"The next time Judy and Stink visit."

"The next time Judy and Stink visit."

"And it will be just as fun as Elmer."

"And it will be just as fun as Elmer," said Grandma Lou.

"When we get back to the house, we'll write it down on paper and you can sign it in blood," said Stink.

"Will ketchup do?" asked Grandma Lou.

"Stink, she can just spit to make it official."

"Tell you what," said Grandma Lou. "How about a pinkie handshake?"

"A three-way pinkie promise?" asked Judy.

"A triple-pinkie swear!" said Stink.

"It'll be our very own secret handshake," said Grandma Lou.

Each of them stuck out a little finger.

The three locked pinkies. "Triple dare pinkie swear!" they said all together.

Grandma Lou's eyes danced. "That should seal the deal." She gave them one last sideways squeeze before turning the kayak around. "Pugsy and I look forward to it."

"So, Grandma Lou," said Stink, "got any plans for next weekend?"

Stuff to Do in a Big Bad Blackout:

1. Read a book by candlelight, torch or headlamp.

2. Break out a board game or a pack of cards.

3. Tell not-so-scary scary stories. And knock-knock jokes.

4. Get a piece of string or wool. Tie it into a loop and play cat's cradle.

5. Shine a torch onto a wall and make shadow puppets with your hands. *Quack, boo, hippety-hop!*

SCREAM LIKE A MONKEY

WILD CARD ?

JUMP 4 <···SPACES

SKIP 3 SPACES

PICK A CARD

EXTRA TURN

LOSE A TURN

WIN!

START

PICK A CARD

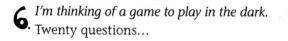

6. *I'm thinking of a game to play in the dark. Twenty questions…*

7. Play the Quiet Game. See who can last the longest without a peep, squeak or giggle.

8. Get your Picasso on. Draw a picture in the dark (no peeking!) and see if family and friends can guess what your masterpiece is.

9. Say a name that rhymes with twister. Oops – that's play a game of Chinese whispers!

BONUS CARD

RETURN TO START!

EXTRA TURN

PICK A CARD

WILD CARD

SKIP 3 SPACES

WILD CARD ?

ROLL AGAIN!

BONUS